W9-DFA-255

PRINCESS UNLIMITED

Jacob Sager Weinstein   ILLUSTRATED BY Raissa Figueroa

CLARION BOOKS
Houghton Mifflin Harcourt
Boston   New York

Clarion Books
3 Park Avenue
New York, New York 10016

Clarion Books is an imprint of Houghton Mifflin Harcourt Publishing Company.

hmhbooks.com

The illustrations in this book were done digitally.
The text was set in Adobe Jenson Pro.
Cover design by Kaitlin Yang
Interior design by Sharismar Rodriguez and Kaitlin Yang

Library of Congress Cataloging-in-Publication Data is available.
ISBN 978-1-328-90474-4

Manufactured in China
DC 10 9 8 7 6 5 4 3 2 1
4500827343

For Ammi-Joan Paquette, who regularly rides into battle
armed with a contract —J.S.W.

For those who don't mind getting their shoes dirty —R.F.

Princess Susan lived in a castle high atop a hill,
in a room filled with sparkles and frilly dresses.

But down below, the
kingdom had a problem.
A dragon problem.

"Why don't you buy the knights swords, instead of making them use hedgehogs and drinking straws?" the princess asked.

"I spent all the royal gold on sparkles and frills," said the king. "A princess needs frills."

"They help her look fancy," agreed the queen.

"I don't need to look fancy," the princess said. "I need to help the kingdom. Let me earn more gold."

But the king and the queen weren't listening.

"Pssst!" whispered Eleanor the scullery maid. "There's a job opening in the kitchen."

They scrubbed all day, until the pots and pans shone like mirrors.
But when it was time to pay the princess . . .

"I'm sorry," said the chef. "All we have in the treasury is a moth, a used toothbrush, and more lemons than I can count."

"Hmmmm . . ." said Princess Susan.

"Ice-cold lemonade for sale! Can't face the fiery breath of a dragon without a nice cold lemonade!"

"We sold two hundred thirteen pitchers of lemonade, plus four cups," Princess Susan told her parents.

"That explains all the gold in the treasury," said the queen.

"We used it to buy more sparkles," said the king. "Princesses need sparkles."

"They help her glitter," the queen agreed.

"What!??" yelled Eleanor. "That gold was for pokey, pointy things, not spangly, shiny things! You'll never defeat the dragon now."

The crowd gasped. It was a crime for a scullery maid to talk back to the king.

But the king and the queen still weren't listening.

Princess Susan told Eleanor, "I'm promoting you to Vice Princess of Brave Truth Telling. And we're going to save this kingdom ourselves."

They set off the next day.

"Dragons love kidnapping princesses in frilly dresses," warned Vice Princess Eleanor.

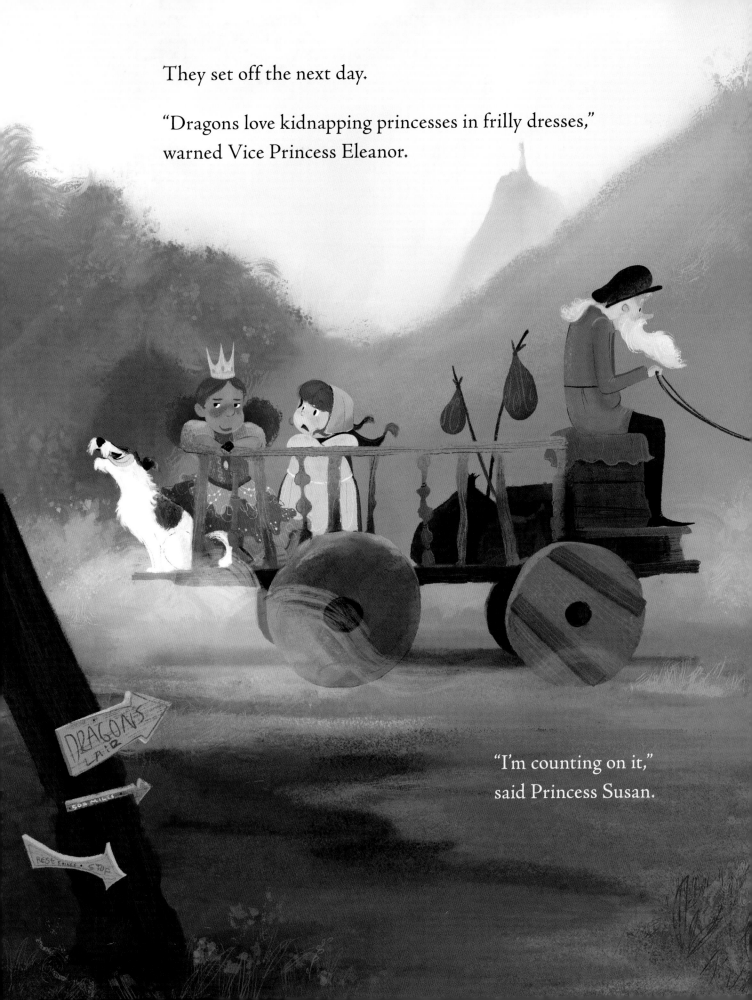

"I'm counting on it," said Princess Susan.

As they rode, they passed knights
going to fight the dragon . . .

and coming back.

Princess Susan and Vice Princess Eleanor
were almost at the dragon's cave when . . .

. . . the dragon attacked.

The princess threw a handful
of sparkles into the air.

They reflected
the dragon's flame
like a thousand tiny stars.

Blinded, the dragon crashed into a rock wall

and fell.

"Wait!" cried Vice Princess
Eleanor. "You'll never kill
the dragon without a sword."

"Nobody is getting killed today,"
Princess Susan answered.
She reached into her scabbard
and pulled out . . .

. . . a contract.

"I'd like to offer you a job," she told the dragon. "You'll be able to buy all the sparkles and frilly dresses you want, without having to kidnap a single princess."

"Hook your house up to the Dragon Fire
Network! Get a dragon-fire fireplace and
never haul a load of wood again!"

And before long, Princess Susan was well on her way to rebuilding the kingdom.

"How did you afford this?" the king asked.

"My partners and I sold three thousand two hundred and ninety-four Dragon Fire Network subscriptions, plus ten one-week trials," Princess Susan said.

Her parents looked at each other in amazement—
and ran off.

The Vice Princess of Brave Truth Telling called
after them, "You *never* listen . . ."

. . . But this time,
they *had* listened.

And they had a present
for their daughter.

"A princess needs business cards," the queen said.

"They help her run her own business," the king agreed.

PRINCESS SUSAN

Head Princess
PRINCESS UNLIMITED

MAX

Chief Sock Eater
PRINCESS UNLIMITED

ELEANOR

Vice Princess of
Brave Truth Telling
PRINCESS UNLIMITED

WYVERN

Senior Dragon for
Flame Provision
PRINCESS UNLIMITED